The Castle in the Field

Michael Morpurgo

The Castle in the Field

With illustrations by

Faye Hanson

Barrington Stoke

First published in 2013 in Great Britain by
Barrington Stoke Ltd
18 Walker Street, Edinburgh, EH3 7LP

www.barringtonstoke.co.uk

Text © 1974 Michael Morpurgo
Illustrations © Faye Hanson

ISBN: 978-1-78112-287-7

Printed in China by Leo

This book has dyslexia friendly features

To the children and teachers of Wickhambreaux School where this story was first told

Contents

Chapter 1
Buckets

We couldn't go home after school
because there was no one there. Mum
worked in the village shop and didn't
get back till five. Dad never came home
until much later. He worked on the
farm, driving tractors and looking after
the cows, and he was never home till
after supper.

The three of us were walking home – my younger sister Lisa, my friend Tom and me. We stopped at the end of the lane to wait for Mum.

"It's going to rain, Chris, I can feel it," said Tom.

And he was right. It began to bucket down. It was the kind of rain that really hurt when it hit you – it stung your face and neck.

We were all soaked through within a minute. We tried to shelter behind the hedge, but that didn't help because the rain was coming straight down. Already the ditches were running water, and it wouldn't stop.

"The shelter, what about the shelter?" Tom yelled over the rain. Tom was my best friend at school and always came home with us. He looked like a half-drowned rat with his black hair laid flat on his head and his nose running like a tap.

"We're not allowed in there," Lisa yelled. She was holding her schoolbag over her head.

Tom didn't listen to Lisa. He ducked under the hedge and across the muddy field. We followed him, bumping up and down in the furrows, squelching and slithering our way to the shelter.

Chapter 2
The Pill-box

Lisa got there first and pulled the door open. We all crept in, dripping and sodden. It wasn't really a shelter – it was an old army guard post meant for soldiers to use if the Germans had invaded in World War Two.

It was called a pill-box because it was the same shape as the bottles medicine used to come in. That's what Dad said, anyway. I thought it was more like the shape of a 20p piece, with slits in the walls for the soldiers to fire guns through.

The pill-box was on old Mr Rafferty's land. He was a mean old codger who disliked everyone, and children even more. He'd stuck a sign that said 'Trespassers will be prosecuted' outside the pill-box.

We sat on our schoolbags and dripped.

"It's strange in here," Lisa said. She shook her head like a dog after a swim.

"I've always wanted to come in here," said Tom. "Look – you can see for miles from these windows."

I was ferreting around in the dark,
slimy corners. I turned over old damp
sacks and rusty cans while Lisa sat there
and complained about how wet she was.

I was about to step up to have a look
with Tom, when my foot kicked a round
steel thing. It rolled off across the hut
and crashed into the other side by Lisa.

"Watch out! That nearly hit me!"
She picked it up. "Yuck! It's all slimy."
The thing fell to the floor with a clatter.

I picked it up. "It's a soldier's
helmet!"

Tom grabbed it. "It must have been
here since World War Two," he said.
"There's a hole in the top of it – bullet it
looks like."

He put the tin hat on. You should have seen him standing there in this dirty old war hat ten sizes too big.

Lisa and I just fell about laughing.

Well, that's how it all started. We swore on our mothers' graves that we would never tell anyone else about it and never to bring anyone else there. We named it 'The Castle' and went off home.

Chapter 3
The Castle

In the next few weeks we did the Castle up. We made a rule that there must always be one of us on look-out duty in case old Rafferty came along. But he never did.

We cleared out all the old smelly muck, the sacks and tins, and lots of rusty broken tools. Over half-term we swept it all out and brought in some old furniture I found in the loft above the tractor sheds.

Tom managed to bring in two old pictures which Lisa propped up against the wall.

We rolled a bale of straw across the field from the farm and spread it out as a carpet. Then we were moved in, so to speak.

Tom's tin hat hung on a nail above the door in a place of honour and we both brought in all the war-time relics we could lay our hands on.

Dad said the Battle of Britain had been fought in the sky near us and we were always finding bullets and bullet cases and bits of metal that looked like they came from the War.

Tom had a rusty old chunk of metal which he swore was the propeller blade of a German Heinkel plane. I suppose it could have been.

Lisa scrubbed down a wobbly table Mum had thrown out and we had logs for chairs. It became a home from home for all of us.

After we were let out from school, we'd split up and go three different ways, to make sure that no one followed any of us.

We'd meet up on the edge of the
wood by the field and then run across,
bent down. It wasn't far – 30 yards or so,
that's all – but it was open country for
miles around.

We called it 'No Man's Land' and we
worked out a system of signals to make
sure no one left the cover of the wood
until it was all clear. Three whistles
meant 'all clear', one meant 'wait'. It
worked.

Chapter 4
Panic

For over two years the Castle was a well-kept secret.

It was the sheep that nearly gave us away the first time.

About lambing time, old Rafferty put some sheep to grass in the field round the Castle. We were careful of course, and we never crossed 'No Man's Land' unless the sheep were on the other side of the field. Sheep panic, you see.

Well, we'd been in the Castle no more than ten minutes or so one night, and Lisa was getting the tea out of the tin. Then all of a sudden there was a shrill bleating just outside. Lisa dropped the tin and it exploded on the floor, throwing biscuits and cake all over the place.

Tom was on look-out. He rushed to the window nearest the noise.

The bleating went on.

We craned our necks to see out the window and discovered the reason for the noise, right up against the wall of the Castle. It was a new-born lamb, all black in the face and wobbly, and bleating for its mum. One of its legs was caught in some wire, and the poor thing was letting everyone in the county know.

Of course, its mum came trotting over with the whole flock behind her. They set up a bleating that would have drowned out a brass band.

Tom waved a hand out of the window. "Shoo!" he yelled. "Push off! Go on, get away! Shoo!"

One or two timid sheep moved off and then before we could do anything else, Lisa shouted out.

"Get down! It's old Rafferty. He's coming, he's coming from the barn." We all crouched under the window. "He's got his dog with him as well," Lisa whispered.

"The door!" I said. "What about the door?" Tom pushed the door shut and I rammed the bolt across and fell back under the window, panting. My heart was racing, and I closed my eyes so hard that I saw those odd blobs of light.

Rafferty's steps were right outside now.

"Please God," Lisa whispered.

"Now then, now then, off you go!" we heard Rafferty say. "Whoooaa, what've we got 'ere? Is it yours, Jessie? Come on then, little fellow, out you come. I'd better move that wire, hadn't I? You're all right then now, aren't you?"

The bleating went off into the distance, and we heard old Rafferty coughing as he made his way back across the field. Then came the scratches and whines at the door.

I'd forgotten about the dog. I bit my knuckle and prayed even harder. We heard him sniffle round. And then, after the longest minute I've ever spent, there was a whistle and old Rafferty called, "Come on, boy, what're you up to over there? Come 'ere, boy!" And he went.

Thank God! We all breathed again.

Chapter 5
All Good Things

But I suppose it couldn't last for ever, and it didn't.

In the winter after that spring we had snow on the ground for over three weeks.

Tom got hold of an old oil heater and
Lisa fixed old sacks over the windows
to keep out the cold. We had a candle
on the table. It was glowing and warm
inside while the wind whistled round the
Castle.

I was on look-out, peeping through
a hole in the sacks. It was white
everywhere. There was steam curling
out like a mist from the cow sheds, and
the barn roof was half snow, half tiles.

The door flew open behind me. All I could see was a pair of wellies and some dirty blue jeans. Tom was on his feet now.

"What do you want, Jimmy?" he demanded. "No one asked you in."

Jimmy Tyler came into the Castle, followed by the Bushell brothers. They had left the school the year before and no one had been sorry to see them go. Once they had locked Paula from the Infants in the playground loos.

It was nearly lunchtime before anyone realised she was missing. Mrs Morton heard her and let her out, but you should have seen her, Paula, I mean. She was trembling all over, really terrified.

"What a little nest you've got here," Jimmy said. "But you're not allowed in here, are you? Old Rafferty'd roast you if he knew. Perhaps we'll tell him, won't we, eh?"

Jimmy's cronies laughed in the doorway. Then Jimmy saw the hat above the door.

"Playing soldiers, are we then?" he sneered. "If you're such clever soldiers you don't want to leave your tracks everywhere, do you then?"

"No one asked you here, Jimmy," I said. "You go or we'll kick you out." I was quite surprised at myself. I wasn't brave or anything, just angry – angry that we'd been discovered, angry that Jimmy was making fun of us and the Castle.

Tom was bigger than me and could look very nasty when he chose to. He took a step towards Jimmy. The two Bushells had backed out and Jimmy looked from Tom to me and then to Lisa, who had a hammer in her hand. They went off jeering.

"Now what?" said Lisa. "Jimmy is bound to tell Rafferty."

"Let's get out quick," I said. "In case they tell him now."

Chapter 6
Blockade

We packed our things together – as much as we could, anyway. We were almost ready when there was a loud crash against the door.

"Get out of that if you can, soldier boys!"

It was Jimmy.

"Use a grenade or something! We'll come and see how you are next week!" They ran off, laughing and shouting.

Tom looked out of the window while I tried the door. It was blocked.

"They've put a huge great log against it," Tom said. "We'll never budge it. Never."

We tried one by one, and all together, but there was no shifting it.

The wind dropped. The world outside went grey over the snow. We knew we'd have to call for help, and we knew what it would mean.

"It's no use, Chris," Lisa said. "We'll have to call. Mum'll be home by now and she'll wonder where we've got to."

Tom started to call out of the window towards the barn.

"Help! Help!"

It sounded muffled and quiet. The snow seemed to eat his words. We tried together.

Nothing.

No one came and no one seemed to be moving at old Rafferty's place.

"What about the candle?" Tom said. His voice was hoarse with shouting. "If they can't hear us, perhaps they'll see us."

"There's not much of it left," Lisa said. But we tried. The candle flickered and sputtered up by the window, throwing queer, moving shadows over the Castle's walls. Then that went out. But just as it did so, we heard the crunch of boots in the snow, coming across the field from the woods.

The log was knocked away and the door pulled open. We waited inside, scared and cold, wondering what we'd say to old Rafferty. A torch beam cut the darkness and blinded us.

"Are you all right, Tommy lad?"

It wasn't old Rafferty. It was Mr Bushell from down Tom's lane.

"They told me what they'd done, my boys did," he said. "I'll give them a right going over an' all. And I'll give young Jimmy Tyler a piece of my mind, you see if I don't." He shone his torch around.

"You shouldn't be in here, y'know," he said. "You'd best go on home. You come along with me, Tom, and you two get straight off home. No hanging about now. It's past six, and there'll be more snow."

Chapter 7
Done

Mum was cross and Dad was livid angry. Only Lisa's cat Snug seemed to want us home.

We never went back to the Castle. It wasn't really ours any more. Tom went back some time after and said the place was full of sheep hurdles.

The helmet was still there. He's got it hanging on his bedroom door now.

But it doesn't look quite right.

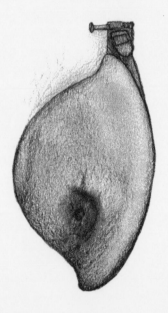

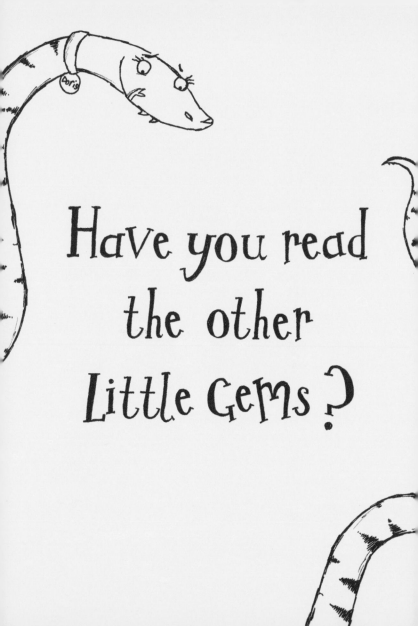

Have you read
the other
Little Gems?